# GILLESPIE TOWN

**Books By Yvonne M Phillip**

*Adult Short Stories*
*Gillespie Town*

*Children's Books*
*Motorcycle to the Moon*

# GILLESPIE TOWN

## Yvonne M Phillip

**Eabhmari Publishing**

GILLESPIE TOWN

Copyright © 2024 by Yvonne Maria Phillip

Cover Photo © Yvonne Maria Phillip

ISBN: 978-1-7380577-0-2

ASIN: 17380577

Eabhmari's paperback edition / January 2024
Eabhmari Publishing, Jane/Finch Mall, 3975 Jane Street RPO, PO Box 21192, Downsview, Ontario, M3N 3A3

*To those going through struggles, trying to find their way.*

## *Gillespie Town*

Flat brown earth, burnt dry, and crying for rain, is stretched out for miles and miles on either side of a long and dusty road. With no moisture flowing from the cracked ground nor falling from the enormous white clouds above to sustain them, small shrubs fell limply like ragdolls held loosely by the waist.

No cool wind has blown over this piece of land in almost a year nor has any passed through the town some fifty miles away to the north. Only a relentless breeze, more inclined to steal than to give breath.

The people of Gillespie Town looked up daily for any sign of rain. Each time they did, hope shone from the eyes of many. However, to the more skeptical, such vivid splendor, such blueness of sky and brightness of clouds were mocking reminders of better times.

Like a mother with her children, the land had once given itself lovingly and unselfishly to the occupants, providing them with everything necessary for a happy life, that was, until almost a year ago when the heavens dried up.

Strangers to Gillespie Town travelled along a dirt road spread through the center of town like a royal carpet of welcome. As they got farther into town, visitors saw that the road divided, forked off to the east and west, while the main artery continued on through the length of the town.

On either side of the main road stood two-storied buildings like soldiers on guard; their wide windows and wide balconies looked down at guests as they passed by.

In one of the few houses in Gillespie Town, Teresa Kohl, twenty-five, was preparing to go out. She swept back the blue lace curtains and looked up at the sky to see the position of the sun. *Good.* It sat high in the sky, ensuring that there would be enough daylight left for her purposes today.

Teresa looked over her shoulder at Mark, her sleeping five-year-old son, before letting the curtains fall into place.

A wave of anxiety swamping her, Teresa gasped and covered her mouth with one hand to bind anymore utterances. If today's outing didn't prove fruitful—Teresa looked down at her feet encased in mauve walking boots, brought her hands into view, and opened and closed them several times. Her baby had been suffering a slow decline in health, and she, a skilled healer had not been able to lift a finger to help.

Teresa turned to watch him as she gathered her shoulder length, chestnut-red hair and pinned it up into a bun. As usual, she was afraid to take her eyes off of him for longer than necessary lest the worse happened. Six months ago, she had thought that she was living the worse case scenario. Now, she knew better.

It was torturous when she had to go out without him; yet, on the rear occasions Teresa ventured out and had to bring him with her, as now, she hesitated to do so. But...

With a resigned sigh, Teresa secured him to her chest in a sling carrier the way a friend had shown her when Mark was a baby. Then, the knowledge was welcomed; today, it was a Godsend. Even though the contrivance was meant for carrying infants, Teresa had modified it for Mark's weight and height now.

With a deep breath for calm and fortification, Teresa pulled on her gloves and left the house.

∧∧∧∧∧∧

Teresa, wearing an ankle-length navy-blue skirt and a white blouse, crossed from the opposite walkway from the empty inn on her way to her buggy. She could feel the stares of Gillespie's people follow her.

During the last few months, they had resorted to staring at her when she went out, apparently as tired of castigating her as she was of explaining herself. Of defending against what she couldn't quite say was a baseless accusation.

Words, as well as herbs were her stock in trade, and the people's constant hostility was a regular reminder that she, more than anyone, needed to mind what she said since, connected to her skills, her words carried more weight than the average person's. Teresa said traditional prayers when she doctored because she found that they manifested the results she wanted. Yet in a moment of strong emotions, Teresa had spoken carelessly—

"Morn' Mrs. Kohl." John North, a crop farmer, exited the general store. When he stopped to talk with her Teresa was careful not to let him see her start of surprise.

She raised her chin higher and held Mark closer. "Mr. North."

He fell into step with her as she gave a nod of acknowledgement and kept on walking. As they walked, Teresa saw a handful of people she had treated for general ailments, all she was able to do at the time. She tried to catch their eye, but each person averted their faces. Although some did not share the view of the majority, they were reluctant to stand with her. The few people who would have stood with Teresa had left town shortly after the drought began.

Many of those who remained in Gillespie Town held her responsible for this drought that plague them. Some of the more hardline religious and superstitious town members followed her and Mr. North, the sound of their collective breath like a living entity at her back and the base of her skull, an otherworldly vocalization of what they left unsaid.

When she and Mr. North reached the stables, Teresa nodded to the stablehand and ignored his slight hesitation before he began to harness her two chestnut-coloured horses to her buggy; because, in the end, she paid her coins just like everyone else. Teresa led the horses outside.

Mr. North was still there, along with a few more town's people. He spoke again. "Mrs. Kohl... I..." He removed his broad-brimmed straw hat as his gaze fell on the child. "Do you soon see an end to this weather? A few months perhaps?"

"No, Mr. North," she said. "I do not see an end to this drought within a few months."

Mr. North twisted his hat within his hands. "You can't do this to us, Mrs. Kohl. Think of your son."

As she felt people's hostility rise and radiate toward her, Teresa breathed deeply of the overheated air, stood a little straighter. Attempting to regain control of her rising temper, she looked down at her son's curly head of black hair. At last, she was able to look at Mr. North with a calm she was far from feeling. "That is all I can do, Mr. North. I realize—"

"You predicted this drought soon after you arrived!" Teresa turned and stared at the speaker. The woman took a step backward. Teresa held in the sigh that fought to pass her lips, the ire leaving her as quickly as it had arisen. *Apparently, not everyone was done pointing fingers.*

Knowing that anything else she said would fall on deaf ears, Teresa turned with deliberate care away from the woman to Mr. North and looked at him for a long moment. Then she climbed into the buggy and carefully picked up the reins.

"Should you not awake the child, Ma'am?" he asked.

Mr. North had been one of her last patients in Gillespie. And one of the few who realized that the words she spoke during healing could prove to be prophetic. He had been running a high fever, and if Teresa had not drudged up the courage to act, to fight past the barrier that had held her incapable of helping her own son, John North might have been her first casualty in her adopted hometown.

Teresa was not about to let her son take up that title. She bent down and whispered to Mr. North.

Those from their impromptu entourage, thinking that she whispered her answer about the drought, leaned forward trying to hear. Teresa sat up and her eyes sparkled for a moment as the group visibly straightened with her; then just as quickly, her eyes clouded over. *Don't do this.*

She blinked rapidly to keep the tears at bay and looked down at Mark before meeting Mr. North's earnest gaze. "My child cannot be awakened, Mr. North. As your fields, my life has also suffered from this drought."

A collective gasp arose from the crowd.

With a click of her tongue, Teresa steered the horses southward, fully aware that the people of Gillespie Town gazed after her.

Mr. North turned to the crowd and spoke wearily, "No, the child is not dead." He placed his hat on his head and walked away.

∧∧∧∧∧∧

Teresa travelled south out of town, instincts leading her. She had ignored them for so long that she was afraid that she might be reading them wrong. However, she pushed through the doubts and kept on going. Eventually she came to the parched land outside of Gillespie.

Teresa walked around, bending on occasion to examine some of the plants. When she found the ones she searched for, excitement and hope bubbled up within her. Teresa tapped them down with large doses of caution.

Hope was such a fragile thing. She had seen how too much of it with little result could turn the heart, sometimes the essence of some people, making them bitter. It had almost happened to her, still could so easily happen to her.

When Mark first took ill, Teresa had been so sure she could heal him; she soon realized that she was dealing with more than a common ailment. And in that moment, because Mark's illness had been so new, so frightening, Teresa had been struck by a type of paralysis that had rendered her incapable of remembering, much less using generations of healer knowledge. Teresa had turned to the medical professionals, had put more faith in the medicines of the day, in the doctors, than in her own knowledge of healing, only to realize that they were as clueless as she was when it came to the Mysterious illness.

Worry and exhaustion had taken over when doctor after doctor could not provide answers about her son's illness. Then she had arrived in Gillespie Town. Small, prosperous, Teresa had thought it a perfect place to care for Mark.

During her first weeks in Gillespie, the people were cautiously friendly and had started coming to her for medical treatment. By then, Teresa had scarcely trusted herself to use even conventional methods of healing. Then the drought came. When it gave no sign of ending, the anxious town's people looked for a reason, and even though people went to her for medical care, most had settled on her as the cause, a widowed woman with a child, who barely left the house, for their unhappiness, for their town's slow slide out of prosperity and into despair.

Feeling isolated and frightened for her child's life, Teresa had spoken from a place of hurt, of despair of her own. She had spoken words uncharacteristic to her nature, words meant to wound, words she wished she could take back, and not only because soon after they had returned to haunt her. Seemingly overnight the drought was upon them, and her son had slipped away from her into unconsciousness.

Teresa swallowed, cradled Mark's head close. If she…lost Mark—she didn't want to lose herself too. Teresa took a deep breath, held, then released it slowly. She was not going to. Teresa was determined to save her child and, by God's grace, herself.

Until Mr. North. Until she had healed him, Teresa had not been sure that she could do it— reconnect with herself, her training, or push pass the barrier that had held her immobile to use her skills. However, after what she had done for Mr. North, Teresa had found that by focusing on one thing at a time, by doing the smallest of things when she felt capable, had added more and more to her confidence.

After she had healed Mr. North, Teresa had studied every medical text she could get her hands on, had kept some, and discarded some of the information she had learned from her reliance on the doctors. And now she was here in a land that was insignificant to most, but not to her. She had at last come back to herself, and her roots. Teresa prayed that a combination of her recently acquired knowledge and the knowledge passed down to her through the generations would restore her son to health. She placed a kiss on top of his head, climbed back into the buggy, and headed back to town.

∧∧∧∧∧

As though the conversation between Mr. North and Teresa, and the public confrontation had acted as catharsis, the people of Gillespie Town began to go out more and more into the scorching heat. Even though it still hadn't rained, Gillespie Town was more active than it had been in months, once again coming to life.

Ladies with handheld fans walked along the boarded sidewalks. Men lazed in saloons. Cries of 'Hello,' and 'How are you?' rang out around the town as people went on with daily life a little lighter than they had done in previous months.

∧∧∧∧∧

A week after her confrontation with the town's people, and after making several trips between the parched land and the town, Teresa Kohl finished setting up everything she needed to revive her child. At last, she was ready, ready to again follow her instincts, ready to put generations of family wisdom to use to revive her baby. In the face of fear, she had neglected herself and the collective information of the skilled healers who came before her. *No longer*.

Teresa entered the land of the limp shrubs and began to administer to Mark on more than a rudimentary level.

Just before she had come out here, some of Gillespie's people had made inquiries about Mark's health, all without asking about the drought. Their apparent kindness had filled her with conflicting emotions, and she had blinked away the moisture that had formed in her eyes. Tears were a luxury she could not afford.

∧∧∧∧∧

Once again alone with her sick child, Teresa called upon her knowledge about herbal medicine and healing and incorporated information from her recent experience and studies to tend to Mark. She created ointments, made healing drinks with her small supply of water and collection of plants, and she prayed.

∧∧∧∧∧∧

Several weeks later in the middle of the night after a day in which the battle between hope and despair was particularly brutal, Teresa awoke to the sound she feared she would never again hear. Thunder.

Deep within her being, Teresa embraced the rumble like a friend, long absent, now returned with all of life's answers.

For days now, the skies had not been so bright a blue, the clouds no longer as white. Instead, the air was rich with the feel and sent of moisture, and she had ingested a bit more of that endless supply of hope that infused this land.

Teresa checked on Mark. He was still unconscious, but his pallor had improved, becoming healthier over the past weeks.

Teresa went to look outside. Dark clouds scuttled against the midnight blue sky. Thunder sounded again so loud that it shook the ground, and the air around her sizzled.

∧∧∧∧∧∧

Two days later, Teresa was again looking out of the tent when the weather broke. Lightning streaked across the sky, and with one especially loud boom of thunder, the now overfilled clouds burst open; a torrent of rain fell, hitting with heavy strikes against the earth and the tents. Teresa closed her eyes and let out a pent-up sigh. Her head bowed. Her instincts had again won out.

In the distance the horses whinnied. Earlier, Teresa had fed and brushed them down. Then she had led them into the second tent she had brought for their shelter. Now, she could only pray that they remained safe.

∧∧∧∧∧

A rustling sound behind her had Teresa turning, just before she turned completely to face the sound, Teresa stood still, trying hard to taper down the elation that struggled to overpower her.

*Mark?* Her heart pounded rapidly causing a physical pain.

*What if it wasn't? What if...?*

*But what else could it be?*

She took a fortifying breath, finished turning, and looked across the tent to where her son lay. The blanket he was lying under twitched, and the rustle sounded again with the movement. An incoherent sound left Teresa's lips; her breath caught and held.

Slowly, Teresa took a step forward, then another, and another. Each one was laborious and yet buoyant as if gravity and levity fought with her feet.

At last, she reached the blanket. Teresa stood looking down at her child, then slowly bent down until she was on her knees beside him. She watched him for any sign of movement. But through long moments that seemed to stretch for eternity, Mark remained still. Her eyes blinked rapidly, and she closed them, felt the push of hot liquid against her lashes.

"Mark." The sound was anguished. Still with her eyes closed, she reached out, moved her fingers to the blanket, slid them up. They came to rest at a spot on his chest.

"My heart."

*Was his breathing deeper?* She asked herself the question even as her fingers rose up, and up with the movement of his torso which was rising higher than it had in months. Her fingers moved down. *Mark*!

Teresa pressed her palm flat, gently, to feel more of the deep rise and fall motions of his breathing. The ragged sound washed over her, and the tears she had fought so hard against over this last year slipped out from between her lashes.

21

Teresa moved her hand up and over the folded edge of the blanket: touched Mark's chin, his nose.... Her cheeks now wet as though she'd stepped out into the downpour, Teresa opened her eyes just as her son's lashes fluttered against his cheeks.

Mark's mouth moved as though formulating words. Then his eyes opened. Unfocussed. They closed and opened several more times. By the time they opened and finally focused on her, Teresa had dried her eyes and her face. Beaming with joy, Teresa gently caressed both hands over his face and hair.

As she looked into her son's beautiful green eyes now bright with recognition, she said, "Hello, Mark."

^^^^^^

After the rain came and the people of Gillespie Town saw that it was not a fluke, that the year-long drought had finally ended, Gillespie Town was once again on the road to regaining prosperity.

The slow awakening that had started with the conversation between Mr. North and Teresa, and the confrontation, had continued. The population increased regularly, starting with the return of some of those who had left during the drought, along with an influx of new citizens.

Existing businesses reopened. New businesses started, with more being built—the sounds of hammering and construction were a regular part of the town long after the drought broke. And to her delight and gratitude, the people of Gillespie Town had again started going to Teresa Kohl for medical treatment.

∧∧∧∧∧∧

Teresa pulled the horses to a stop. The buggy rocked slightly beneath her. Before it came to a full stop, Mark was standing up. Teresa quickly held the reins with one hand and reached behind her with the other. "Mark!"

Teresa drew in a deep breath and released it. Her heart filled as Mark stood and waited for her to come lift him out of the buggy. Teresa was so happy, yet she couldn't help but worry. Mark was still recovering. She was. The town was.

Teresa looked around her; the land was recovering too. Anyone who would have passed through this land six months ago would hardly believe it to be the same place. Now, the land was green and lush. Teresa had affectionately named it,

23

"the Land of The Limp Shrubs." It was those shrubs, a powerhouse of healing herbs in disguise, that had saved her child, made it possible for her to heal him and for Mark to regain his childhood.

Teresa had brought him here to familiarize him with the land and the plants within it. It was not too soon to start teaching him about the family business and his heritage.

Teresa climbed down from the buggy, then lifted Mark to the ground. He gave her a hug then went to explore his surroundings. Teresa glanced at Mark. He ran about while still staying close. He stopped to smell a eucalyptus plant before running again.

Mark didn't talk much, but he was already more insightful than she had been at his age.

Teresa lifted her face to the sky, eyes closed. The sun, once a thing to fear was now a source of joy. She basked in the feel of the sun's rays, its' shine, and warmth on her face, and smiled at the temperate breeze that accompanied them. Both sun and breeze brought succor and peace to Teresa, the land around her, and to the people in the town some fifty miles away to the North.

The End

## About the Author

Yvonne M is a longtime reader. She started writing when she was seventeen. Yvonne M enjoys reading and taking photos of nature. She is also the author of the children's book, "Motorcycle to the Moon." Learn more about her at https://www.yvonnemphillip.com/

Thank you for choosing my book. Please return to your online retailer and leave a review.

Yvonne M.

www.ingramcontent.com/pod-product-compliance
Lightning Source LLC
Chambersburg PA
CBHW071629140626
46555CB00021B/1939